# Masai and I

# and I

by Virginia Kroll

illustrations by Nancy Carpenter

Four Winds Press ❋ New York
Maxwell Macmillan Canada   Toronto
Maxwell Macmillan International
New York   Oxford   Singapore   Sydney

**A note from the artist**
The paintings in this book were done in oil and
color pencil on paper. A special thanks to Angelina,
Gabriella, Jocasta, and Jenny.

For my granddaughter, Olivia Hazel DeAnthony

—V.K.

To Jennie, for getting me started

—N.C.

That day at school, we learned about East Africa and a tall, proud people called the Masai. I feel the tingle of kinship flowing through my veins.

I walk the blocks to my apartment building.
I've met Mrs. Stroud across the hall and the
Johnson family in 4B, but that's all. If I were Masai,
I would have no neighbors who were strangers living
in apartments up and down the halls. Our huts would
sit in a circle around a large animal pen called a
kraal, and everyone would know everyone else.

We always have to wait for Daddy to get home so we can all eat together. If I were Masai, Daddy and Ray would be eating with the other men, and Mama and I with the other women.

Ray goes to the faucet to get some water.
If I were Masai, my brother would walk
long distances to find a water hole, and he
would bring the water back in giant gourds.

"What's for dessert?" I ask.

Mama gives me money to buy some candy bars, and
Ray and I walk to the corner deli. If I were Masai and I wanted
something sweet, I would wait for the honey guide to come.
The little bird would chatter wildly above my head, begging me to follow.
I'd lope along below, and it would lead me to a beehive. I'd light a fire with
sticks rubbed hard together and make a smoking torch to calm the bees. Then
I would scoop the honeycomb and leave enough behind for my friend the bird.

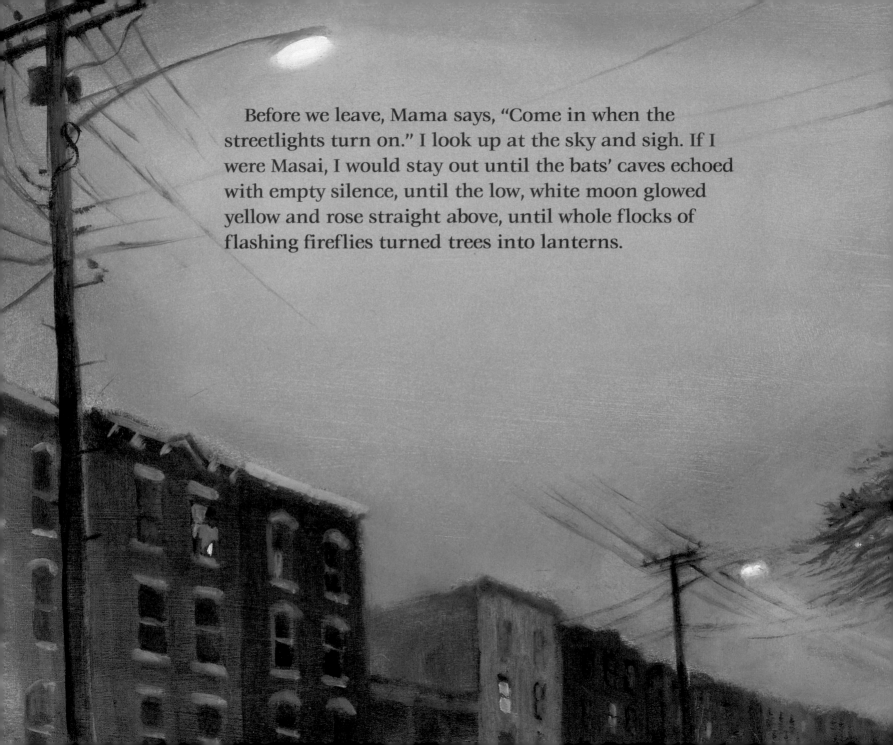

Before we leave, Mama says, "Come in when the
streetlights turn on." I look up at the sky and sigh. If I
were Masai, I would stay out until the bats' caves echoed
with empty silence, until the low, white moon glowed
yellow and rose straight above, until whole flocks of
flashing fireflies turned trees into lanterns.

I would go inside then only to sleep. I would not climb any stairs if I were Masai. I would lift a cowhide flap, and I'd be home.

If I were Masai, I could not look at city
comings and goings from the window in
my room. My hut would have no windows,
only small holes to let out smoke.
We would not have couches, chairs,
lamps, or tables, either—only
several stools.

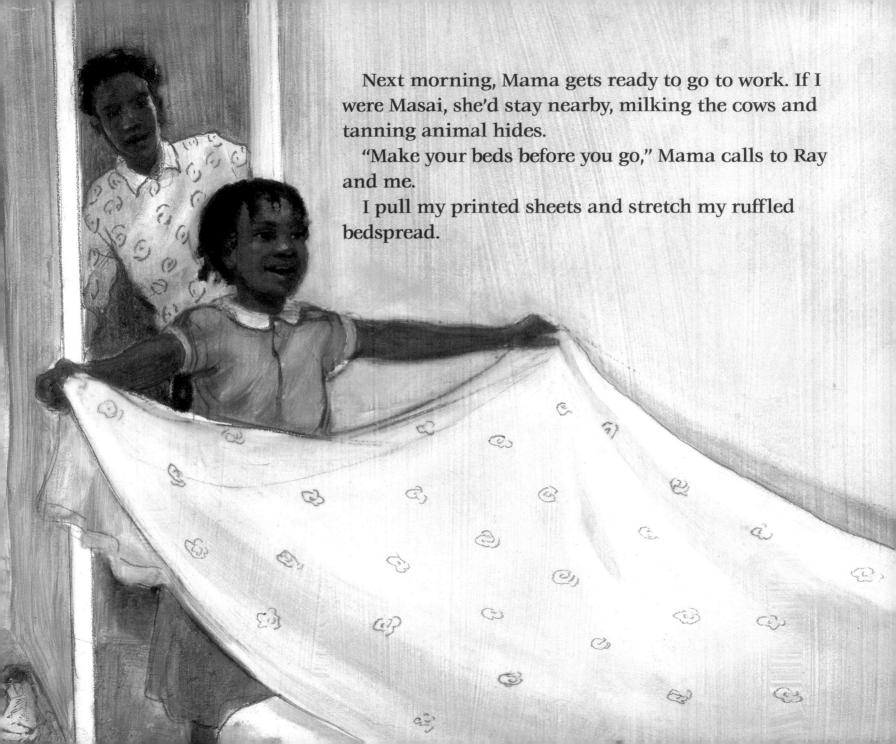

Next morning, Mama gets ready to go to work. If I were Masai, she'd stay nearby, milking the cows and tanning animal hides.

"Make your beds before you go," Mama calls to Ray and me.

I pull my printed sheets and stretch my ruffled bedspread.

If I were Masai, I'd spread a cowhide on the bare earth floor at night and roll it back up in the morning.

I would not have my caged hamster, Huey, if I were
Masai. I would have cows, though, a whole herd, and I'd
know every one by name!

I would not have to go to the zoo to see giraffes or
ostriches, or zebras, either. I'd share the Africa air
with them, the Africa soil,
and the Africa rain.

I set out for school and run back in for my new white sneakers. I almost forgot—I have gym today. If I were Masai, I'd run and leap in bare brown feet across lush green pastures, or pale, parched sod. And only once in a great, great while, I'd wear sandals made of buffalo hide.

That evening, my brother and I fight over who gets the bathroom first. We're going to Grandma's party at the Berries Restaurant. It's her seventieth birthday.

I bathe in scented soap and dry my skin with a thick towel. If I were Masai preparing for a celebration, I'd rub my skin with cows' fat mixed with red clay so that my skin would shine. I'd want to smell nice if I were Masai, just like I do now, so I'd crush sweet-smelling leaves to rub along my shiny skin.

My cousin James comes over, and we pile into the car to drive to the party. If I were Masai, walking three miles would be nothing for me. I'd glide across grasslands, open and free.

Later, when her birthday dinner is over, Grandma stares at me. "My, my, Linda," she says, "how slender and graceful you are. Such a beautiful young girl!"

I kiss her with love and respect, just as I would if I were Masai.

If I were Masai, my name might be Eshe or Hawa or Neema—or even Linde, almost like it is now.

I come home and stare at my reflection in my bedroom mirror...smooth brown skin over high cheekbones and black eyes that slant up a little when I smile. I like what I see. I tingle again with that feeling about kinship. I would look just like this if I were Masai.